Rats on
the Range

RATS ON
THE RANGE

and Other Stories

★

★

JAMES MARSHALL

★

· Dial Books for Young Readers ·

New York

Published by
Dial Books for Young Readers
A Division of Penguin Books USA Inc.
375 Hudson Street
New York, New York 10014

Printed in the U.S.A.
First Edition
Typography by Jane Byers Bierhorst
1 3 5 7 9 10 8 6 4 2

Library of Congress Cataloging in Publication Data

Marshall, James, 1942–1992
Rats on the range and other stories
James Marshall.—1st ed.
p.   cm.
Summary: In eight animal stories the reader
meets a rat family that vacations at a dude ranch,
a pig who takes lessons in table manners, a mouse who keeps
house for a tomcat, and a buzzard who leaves his money
to the Society for Stray Cats—or does he?
ISBN 0-8037-1384-3.   ISBN 0-8037-1385-1 (lib. bdg.)
1. Children's stories, American. [1. Animals—Fiction.
2. Short stories.] I. Title.
PZ7.M35672Rar 1993 [Fic]—dc20 92-28918 CIP AC

"Buzzard's Will" is a playful
tribute to the comedic opera *Gianni Schicchi*
written by Gioachino Forzano, with
music by Giacomo Puccini.

CONTENTS

Miss Mouse

When Thomas J. Cat looked out his window and saw who was standing on his front doorstep, he couldn't believe his tired old eyes. It was a mouse. She was wearing a hat covered with daisies, in one hand she carried a small leather purse, and in the other a wicker suitcase tied up with string. Her skirt was a coarse wool, as it was the dead of winter.

"Dinnertime!" exclaimed Thomas to himself. "She's awfully small, but perhaps I can stretch it out with chopped carrots and celery."

The doorbell rang insistently.

"Yoo-hoo!" called out the mouse.

Thomas J. Cat threw on his bathrobe and opened the door a crack. If she sees I'm a tomcat, she'll scamper away, he thought. And I am much too old and sickly for a chase.

"Who is it?" he called out.

"My name is Miss Mouse," said the mouse. "I've come in response to your advertisement for a housekeeper. I have references."

She began to fumble about in her purse.

The tomcat hadn't the slightest idea what the mouse was talking about.

"This *is* 93 Hollow Road, is it not?" said Miss Mouse.

The tomcat was about to inform her that it was 89 Hollow Road, when he thought better of it.

"Er, yes indeed, 93, that's me," he said.

"May I come in?" said Miss Mouse. "It's chilly out here."

"By all means," said the tomcat, throwing open the door, but remaining behind it.

Miss Mouse stepped over the threshold.

"Why are you standing behind the door?" she said.

"Er," said the tomcat. "I'm ashamed of my appearance."

"I see," said Miss Mouse.

Then she looked about the tomcat's messy living room.

"My, my," she said. "I'll have to start in right away. That is, if I have the job. You won't regret it, I do good work."

The tomcat thought for a minute. Certainly he could use some straightening up around the house. In the past few years he'd really let things slide. And when all the work was finished, *then* he could eat the mouse—around snack time. And he wouldn't even have to pay her a penny.

"Excellent," said the tomcat. "The job is yours."

Miss Mouse inspected the pantry and the area under the sink.

"You have no detergents or cleansers!" she said. "I'll just pop around the corner to the market and buy some things. I'll need about twenty dollars."

The tomcat found a twenty-dollar bill in his robe pocket.

I was planning to spend this at the races, he thought.

Miss Mouse took the twenty.

"I'll be back in a jiffy. Perhaps you can make us a nice pot of tea?"

"By all means," said the tomcat, who'd never made tea in his life.

"And by the way," said Miss Mouse, "I know you're a tomcat, so you can come out from behind that door."

"How could you tell?" said the tom-cat.

"One knows these things," said Miss Mouse. "But I'm sure we'll get along just fine."

Miss Mouse firmly believed that kindness, industry, and generosity of spirit could tame the most ferocious of creatures.

She went out the front door.

"Perhaps I've made a mistake," said the tomcat. "What if she doesn't come back? Ah well, you just have to trust."

He went into the kitchen to try and rustle up some tea.

When Miss Mouse returned, carrying two shopping bags full of detergents and cleansers, she heard a pitiful groaning coming from the kitchen. The tomcat had badly burned his paws while making tea. He was rolling about the floor in considerable pain.

"Dear, oh dear," said Miss Mouse.

"We'll have to attend to this immediately. Fortunately I have a first aid kit in my suitcase."

"Hurry," said the tomcat. "I'm dying!"

Miss Mouse retrieved her first aid kit, applied some soothing ointment to the burned paws, and wrapped them with bandages.

"Snug," she said. "And now you must get into bed and do absolutely nothing. We don't want these paws to become infected. Let me help you to your room."

The tomcat leaned on Miss Mouse, and together they haltingly made their way to the bedroom.

"Holy cow!" cried Miss Mouse. "This is worse than the living room. It will take me *days* to clean."

"I'm somewhat disorganized," said the tomcat, slipping in between the gray sheets.

For the rest of the morning and most

of the afternoon, Miss Mouse worked in the living room.

"Tut, tut, tut," she said. "And cats have the reputation of being so clean and orderly."

She swept out a large ball of fur that had accumulated under the sofa.

At four o'clock the tomcat, who had been dozing and dreaming of all *sorts* of tasty things, was awakened by a gentle tap at his bedroom door.

"Come in," he said.

Miss Mouse came in struggling with a large tea tray piled high with sardine sandwiches and potato chips. There was even a mug of hot cocoa. She sat on the side of the bed and popped the sandwiches into the tomcat's open mouth. "Yum, yum," said the tomcat.

When snack time was over, the tomcat felt all plump and rosy.

"I think I'll go back to sleep now," he said.

"Oh no," said Miss Mouse. "I have to change these filthy bedclothes."

And she put the tomcat, all bundled up, on the back porch while she cleaned and tidied up the bedroom.

She was in the bedroom quite some time and the tomcat grew concerned and went to investigate.

The bedroom smelled of cleanser and room freshener and was as neat as a pin. Miss Mouse was sitting propped up on the bed and absorbed in a thick book.

"I found this on the top shelf in the closet," said Miss Mouse.

"It must have been left by the previous tenant," said the tomcat. "I don't read much myself."

"Well, it's wonderful," said Miss Mouse. "Just listen to this. . . ."

The tomcat sat beside the bed, and Miss Mouse began to read.

It was a story about a treasure ship with billowing sails, a swashbuckling hero, and wicked pirates. An hour later Miss Mouse finished reading.

"And the evil pirate Captain Black-heart was never seen again. The End."

The tomcat, whose pulse was racing, was enchanted.

"More!" he cried.

"We'll read another tomorrow," said Miss Mouse. "I must cook dinner. We're having a tuna casserole."

Days went by and Miss Mouse and the tomcat established a fixed and pleasant routine.

While the tomcat slept late, Miss Mouse tidied up the house, went shopping, and cooked. Every day just after snacks she read a story from the thick book. It was the tomcat's favorite hour. Miss Mouse read thrilling stories about dinosaurs, cowboys, and space explorers. And the tomcat could never get enough.

"Things are working out quite nicely, aren't they?" said Miss Mouse. "I hope you are pleased with my work."

"Indeed," said the tomcat.

But one day Miss Mouse discovered something that shook her to the core of her being. While straightening up once again the tomcat's cluttered bedroom, she spotted a newspaper that was open to the Home Section. It was a full page of recipes of various mouse dishes. Several of the recipes were circled in ink. Miss Mouse had to sit down and catch her breath.

"Really!" she said. "I see my philosophy of kindness and generosity of spirit has not paid off. A cat is still a cat."

She checked the newspaper again, just to be certain she hadn't overlooked something. Perhaps the tomcat was planning to substitute parsnips or potatoes for the mouse meat in the recipe. But no such luck. There in the tomcat's own shaky handwriting was a shocking notation beside this recipe:

MOUSE MOUSSE

Boil a large mouse, as large as you can catch.
Brown an onion.
Place in a blender, turn on to finely chopped, for five minutes.
Scoop out the mixture and place in a buttered pie tin.
Place in the refrigerator overnight. Serves one.

"Yum, yum," the tomcat had written. "I'll have this one for my Easter dinner."

Miss Mouse consulted her calendar. Easter was several weeks away. If she used her wits, she would be able to stay in the snug tidy house a bit longer. On the day before Easter she would—sadly—leave.

The tomcat entered the room and Miss Mouse hurriedly hid the newspaper behind her.

"Shall we read another story?" she said.

"Excellent," said the tomcat. And he settled himself on the bed.

Miss Mouse opened the thick book, but she was disappointed to find that all the remaining stories were about love and romance—entirely unsuitable to be read to a tomcat who loved adventure.

He'll soon grow tired of them, and then there's no telling what he'll do, she thought.

"I'm waiting," said the tomcat.

Miss Mouse cleared her throat and pretended to read. "Once upon a time in a dark and smelly cave, there lived an evil dragon."

"Oh goody," said the tomcat. "This is going to be a hot one."

Miss Mouse continued to make up her story, all the while pretending to read from the book. It was all about a brave knight and how he defeated the evil dragon.

"This is the best of all," said the tomcat.

Weeks passed. Sometimes Miss Mouse told stories that were scary. The tomcat's fur stood on end. Sometimes the tales were creepy.

"Ooh," said the tomcat.

And every day Miss Mouse checked off the calendar.

On the day before Easter, while the tomcat was dozing, Miss Mouse packed up her wicker suitcase, wrote a hurried note, and tiptoed out of the house. At the corner of Cedar and Maple she caught a streetcar for the train station.

When the tomcat awoke, he was miffed at not finding Miss Mouse who always brought in his tea and then "read" him a story. But Miss Mouse was nowhere about. Pinned to the back of the sofa was the following note (in Miss M's neat little handwriting):

Dear Thomas J. Cat,

I know what you are planning to have for your Easter dinner. That is too much of a sacrifice for me to make. So I must save myself. I am leaving.

Yours truly,
Miss Mouse

P. S. There is a casserole in the refrigerator.

"Rats!" cried the tomcat. "She has left me! I wasn't *really* going to eat her!"

But in his heart of hearts he knew the opposite was true.

On the local train to Trenton Miss Mouse gazed out the rain-streaked window. She would pay a visit to her Aunt Tillie before looking for further employment.

"No cats this time," she said out loud, startling the passenger in the next seat.

In the following days the tomcat grew weaker and weaker. He'd gotten used to being waited on, and TV frozen dinners were no longer to his taste. And more to the point, he missed Miss Mouse's stories. (He even may have missed Miss Mouse herself, hard to say.) A day without one of Miss Mouse's stories was a day without sunshine. He tried to make up his own stories, but found it was not so easy to do. "Once upon a time . . ." was as far as he could get. He knew of course that Miss Mouse had been making up her stories for quite some time now. "She always held the book upside down," he said fondly.

To keep the stories in his memory the tomcat wrote them out in a notebook. As his paws were still weak and shaky, it took him several more days. Copying out the stories made him sad, and finally he fell into a swoon.

The doorbell rang, and the tomcat flew to open it. It was Miss Mouse.

"Had enough?" she said.

The tomcat was overjoyed to see her.

"Please come back," he said.

"Things will have to improve," said Miss Mouse. "You must give up eating mouse meat," she said. "And I want it in writing." And she thrust a legal document under his nose for him to sign.

"Anything," said the tomcat.

"Now let's have a nice hot dinner," said Miss Mouse, stepping into the kitchen.

"And then can we have a story?" asked the tomcat.

"Of course," said Miss Mouse.

And that is the end of the story of Miss Mouse and the tomcat. Except that perhaps you'd care to know that the tomcat sent off Miss Mouse's stories to one of the better publishers, who snapped them right up. And with the arrival of Miss Mouse's money from the publisher, they were able to live a far more comfortable life. They were even able to hire full-time help.

When Pig
Went to Heaven

When Miss Lola the new school-teacher came to town, Pig fell head-over-heels in love. Miss Lola was the prettiest, sweetest-smelling pig he'd ever met.

"She's the one," said Pig.

And he asked her for a date. Miss Lola, who was on the shy side, said no. Pig was heartbroken. But every day he sent flowers to the schoolhouse and put his poems in Miss Lola's mailbox. And Miss Lola agreed to a date.

"Next Saturday night at 6:30?" said Pig.

"Fine," said Miss Lola. "I like to eat early."

Pig was overjoyed.

On Thursday Pig stopped by the barber's to have the coarse hairs on his snout trimmed.

"Saturday night, eh?" said the barber. "Where are you taking her?"

"I'm not sure," said Pig.

"I hear Chez Marcel is the best restaurant in town," said the baker, who'd stopped in for his daily shave.

"Then Chez Marcel it is," said Pig.

"Chez Marcel is very fancy," said the barber. "You will have to wear a tie. And I hope your table manners are okay."

Now Pig had never been to a first-class restaurant. He always ate at Porker O'Shaunessy's Hamburger Haven down the road. And he was *always* there when the three-for-one special was on.

"Do you know about the little fork and the big fork?" said the barber.

"There are *two* forks?" asked Pig.

"The small fork is for appetizers or salads," said the butcher.

"I love salads," said Pig.

"Pay attention, Pig," said the baker. "And the bigger fork is for your main course."

"I see," said Pig, who was already confused.

"You will impress Miss Lola if you speak in French," said the barber. "Just a few words will do. Say *Bonjour* to Monsieur Marcel when you arrive (it means 'good day'), and when you are seated, ask for *La carte, s'il vous plaît* (which means 'the menu, if you please')."

"I know that," said Pig.

"I have an idea," said the barber. "Let's do a practice run. We'll pretend this is Chez Marcel."

A card table and two chairs were set up in the middle of the barbershop.

"Now go out and come back in," said the barber to Pig.

"What a great idea," said Pig.

He went outside and came back in.

"Hi, guys!" he said.

"NO, NO, NO!" said the baker. "You must say 'Bonjour, Monsieur Marcel.'"

"Bonjour, Monsieur Marcel," said Pig.

"I think he's got it!" said the barber.

"Now offer Miss Lola the nicest seat," said the baker.

"Miss Lola's not here," said Pig.

"We're *pretending!*" said the barber.

"Oh," said Pig.

All afternoon and most of the next day Pig was instructed in the art of good restaurant manners. With the exception of a few mistakes, Pig seemed to get the hang of it.

"Now comes the hard part," said the barber. "Making interesting and amusing conversation."

"Huh?" said Pig.

"Ladies prefer gentlemen who can keep them amused," explained the barber. "I'll pretend I'm Miss Lola."

And he sat down across from Pig and batted his eyelashes.

"Now say something amusing."

"Er," said Pig. "Do you like brussels sprouts?"

"Oh dear," said the barber. "We have more work to do."

For hours and hours Pig practiced making interesting and amusing conversation.

"Read any good books lately?" said Pig.

"I've just seen the most beautifully written play," said Pig.

"Would you care to hear one of my poems?" said Pig.

"No," said the barber. "Not that."

At 6:30 a taxi pulled up at Miss Lola's house. Miss Lola was ready and waiting and peeking out the window. Pig came to the door, handed Miss Lola a beautiful corsage, escorted her to the taxi, and they were off.

Monsieur Marcel himself greeted them at the door of his restaurant.

"Bonjour, Monsieur Marcel," said Pig.

Miss Lola was impressed.

And Monsieur Marcel gave them the best table in the house.

Pig put his napkin in his lap.

"La carte, s'il vous plaît," he said to the waiter. "That means 'the menu, if you please.'"

"I know," said the waiter.

"Oh Pig," said Miss Lola. "What a lovely place."

"Glad you like it," said Pig. "I come here quite often."

Miss Lola and Pig studied the menu.

"I'll start off with a crisp green salad," said Miss Lola. "And then I'll have the Chef's special."

"Me too," said Pig.

That was easy, he thought.

While dinner was being prepared, Pig tried to make interesting and amusing conversation. At first it was slow going.

"Read any good books lately?"

"Not really," said Miss Lola.

"I just saw the most beautifully written play," said Pig.

"What was it called?" asked Miss Lola.

"I forgot," said Pig.

"Do you have any more of your poems?" said Miss Lola.

Pig was delighted. And until dinner was served, he recited his poetry.

"Ooh," said Miss Lola.

The waiter brought the salads.

"Merci," said Pig.

He was delighted that things were going so well.

Then Pig noticed that Miss Lola had stuck her snout directly into her salad and was noisily munching away. There was a lot of slurping, grunting, and intake of air. Pig picked up his fork.

"I never use forks," said Miss Lola. "They're so silly."

"I agree," said Pig, who'd become adept at using a fork and wanted to show off.

Then Miss Lola dropped some of her lettuce on the floor, picked it up with a swoop, and popped it into her mouth. Other diners couldn't help but notice, and whispered among themselves.

"I'm thirsty," said Miss Lola.

Pig ordered a bottle of mineral water.

"Not the bubbly kind," he said.

When the mineral water was brought, Miss Lola said, "I'll do that." And she bit off the plastic cap.

Later Miss Lola ordered three desserts and devoured them in no time flat. She had gobs of whipped cream all over her snout and some in her ears.

"I liked the eclairs best," she said.

"Have another one," said Pig, who'd brought a lot of money and wasn't worried about the bill.

Miss Lola picked her teeth and burped so loudly that all conversation in the restaurant came to a halt.

At the door of the restaurant Monsieur Marcel said good-bye to them personally.

"Do come again, please," he said. "It's so gratifying to have customers who really know how to enjoy their food."

On the way home Pig asked the driver to pull over and stop.

Then he and Miss Lola got out and had a lovely mud bath in a ditch by the side of the road.

"You really know how to entertain a girl," said Miss Lola.

And Pig was in heaven.

When Pig
Took the Wheel

When Pig received his driver's license, folks about town shook in their boots.

"We're in for it now," said the barber who was standing outside his shop.

"They actually gave Pig a *license*?" asked the pharmacist. "That's insane!"

"What is the world coming to?" said the baker.

Just then they heard a terrific roar, the screeching of brakes, and the grinding of gears.

"Here comes Pig now," said the barber. "Run for your lives!"

They all hurried into the safety of the

barbershop and looked out the window. Around the corner came Pig. He was driving a bright yellow sports car and was leaving a tremendous amount of dust and exhaust behind him.

"Hotcha!" cried Pig to the three in the barbershop.

And he tore off down the street. "Birdbrain!" called out the barber.

A block away Pig narrowly missed hitting an old duck crossing the street.

"Imbecile!" screamed the old duck.

And Pig was gone.

"This town won't be safe as long as Pig is at the wheel," said the baker.

The barber and the pharmacist agreed. Pig was a serious danger to himself and to others.

"I've already given Pig ten speeding tickets," said the sheriff, who'd happened by. "He hasn't paid a single one of them—

just puts them in his glove compartment. If he doesn't pay them soon, he'll end up in the slammer."

"Good place for him," said the barber.

Later that afternoon as the Homer J. Catkins family was sitting down to tea, Pig drove up their driveway, roared past the side of the house, spun around on Homer Jr.'s basketball court, and zoomed back down the driveway.

"Hotcha!" he cried out as he disappeared down the street.

Mr. Catkins's nerves were totally shattered. "What if I'd been gardening by the side of the house? I might have gotten run over."

"And that Pig is such a bad influence on the young," said Mrs. Catkins.

"I want a sports car just like Pig's," said Homer Jr.

"You see," said Mrs. Catkins to her husband. "What did I tell you?"

At the weekly town meeting folks discussed the situation.

"Pig must be stopped," someone said.

Suddenly there came a tremendous roar from outside.

"We know who *that* is," the barber said.

Pig appeared at the door.

"We're glad you're here, Pig," said the chairperson. "This meeting has been called to discuss fast and reckless driving in town. Someone has been abusing his driving privileges and is endangering everyone."

"Shocking!" said Pig. "I *am* glad I came. These things must be stopped. It's unfair when one citizen takes advantage of the others. So selfish and inconsiderate."

"*Really,* Pig!" said the chairperson.

"We're talking about *you!*"

"Well!" said Pig. "Of all the nerve! I know my rights!"

And he stormed out.

"Pig just doesn't get it," the barber said.

The next day Pig was out on one of his joyrides about town. He was driving especially fast and recklessly, taking the corner of Maple and Elm on two wheels and scaring the same old duck half to death.

"They can't slow *me* down," said Pig. The barber, the baker, and the pharmacist stepped back into the safety of the barbershop.

"I hope Pig doesn't head south of town," said the pharmacist. "I just heard the high bridge is out over Gopher's Gulch. And it's a long way down."

"Sharp rocks and boulders," said the barber. "Someone should inform Pig."

Just then Pig roared by.

The barber and the pharmacist tried to flag him down.

Everyone is waving at me, thought Pig. They mustn't be mad anymore.

He waved back.

South of town Pig headed out to Gopher's Gulch to do some fishing. Folks along the way jumped up and down and waved their arms.

"Such nice, friendly types around here," said Pig.

He waved back.

"The high bridge . . ." someone cried, but the rest was drowned out by the roar of Pig's powerful machine. Pig was gone in a cloud of dust and exhaust.

Gopher's Gulch was just around the

next bend. Pig stepped on the accelerator. He was getting closer and closer. With tires screeching he rounded the bend and aimed for the bridge. He was going entirely too fast to read the signs:

BRIDGE OUT!
TURN BACK!
DANGER!

And he crashed right through the wooden barrier.

"Have you heard about Pig?" said the pharmacist.

"Oh no, he didn't!" cried the barber. "Poor, poor Pig. He just wouldn't change. Tell us all the sad details." And he got out his handkerchief and wiped away a tear.

"Oh, Pig's all right," said the pharmacist. "He crashed through the wooden barrier and shot over Gopher's Gulch—or almost. The sports car fell short of the other bank and got smashed on the sharp rocks."

"And Pig?" said the others.

"Pig grabbed onto a branch and was just dangling there until Sheriff Bob rescued him. He's shaken up—scraped his knees, I believe—and is in the hospital for observation."

"I hope he's learned his lesson," said the baker.

Then they heard the sound of what appeared to be a runaway lawn mower approaching the corner.

"At least we know it isn't Pig," said the pharmacist.

But it *was* Pig. He was riding an electric wheelchair. His knees were all bandaged up. And he was going much too fast.

The barber, the baker, and the pharmacist all shook their heads. "Hopeless," said the barber.

They were surprised, however, to see Pig pull up in front of the jailhouse, stop, and get out. Sheriff Bob was waiting at the door.

"Pig has turned himself in!" cried the barber. "We've just seen Pig's last ride."

"Too bad," said the others.

But Pig was out of the jailhouse in a jiffy. He'd paid all his tickets and turned over his license for good. In no time he was back in his wheelchair and zipping down Main Street—just as the old duck was about to cross.

"Hotcha!" called out Pig.

"Hotcha yourself!" screamed the old duck. "I'm leaving this town!"

And he did.

Mouse Party

Miss Mouse was tidying up in the kitchen when her friend the tomcat came in from a stroll.

"See anything interesting today?" said Miss Mouse.

"Maybe," said the tomcat, who loved to tease.

"What? What?" said Miss Mouse, who *hated* being teased. "What did you see?"

The tomcat sat down in his favorite easy chair, unfolded the newspaper, and pretended to read.

"If you don't tell me what you saw, you won't get a story," said Miss Mouse, who knew when to get tough.

"Well," said the tomcat. "It seems that a large family of mice has moved in several blocks away. I saw them carrying in furniture and boxes. And one of them was painting a name on the mailbox."

"Oh?" said Miss Mouse. "Perhaps I know them."

"They're called the Johnsons," said the tomcat. "A common enough name."

Miss Mouse decided she did not know any mice by the name of Johnson.

"I shall invite them to tea for tomorrow afternoon," said Miss Mouse, sitting down at her writing desk and scribbling a quick note.

"Hmm," said the tomcat.

He did not especially relish the idea of having a house full of mice—especially as he'd given up mouse meat. But he didn't want to spoil Miss Mouse's fun.

"Do as you like," he said.

"You'll join us of course," said Miss Mouse.

Maybe they won't miss one or two, thought the tomcat, who was feeling a relapse coming on.

"Not so fast," said Miss Mouse. "*I* know what you're thinking. You must promise to behave. Or else."

"Oh very well," grumbled the tomcat.

"What is the address?" said Miss Mouse, licking closed the envelope.

"Two hundred Hollow Road," said the tomcat.

Miss Mouse wrote the address on the envelope and handed it to the tomcat.

"Be so kind as to drop this off in the Johnsons' box," she said.

The tomcat took the envelope and sauntered out the door.

"I'm trusting you to behave," said Miss Mouse.

The next afternoon at five minutes to four Miss Mouse surveyed her tea table, which was piled high with cucumber and watercress sandwiches, scones, butter, and various jams. She had laid out her best china and silver and had put some roses from the backyard into a vase.

"Now go put on a tie," she said to the tomcat.

"Aww," said the tomcat.

"It's proper," said Miss Mouse.

And the tomcat obeyed.

At four on the dot a hot rod pulled up in front of the tomcat and Miss Mouse's house. There was a lot of shrieking and laughing and carrying on.

Miss Mouse ran to the window.

"Oh no!" she cried.

"Let the good times roll!" someone yelled.

And everyone got out of the hot rod.

"Oh my stars!" cried Miss Mouse, peeking through the curtain.

"What seems to be the trouble?" said the tomcat coming into the room and adjusting his tie.

"They're coming *here!*" cried Miss Mouse. "It's the Johnsons and—gulp— they're *rats*! Great big ugly rats!!"

"They did seem on the large side," said the tomcat.

The Johnsons came to the door, rang the bell, and yelled, "Open up! We're hungry!"

"Are they wearing ties?" said the tomcat.

"No," answered Miss Mouse. "They're shabbily dressed."

"I'll go change," said the tomcat.

The Johnsons rang the bell again and again.

It would be rude not to let them in, thought Miss Mouse. After all, I *did* invite them.

And she opened the door.

"Hi, honey!" said Mr. Johnson. "What took ya so long? Nice place ya got here. Let's eat."

Without bothering to introduce his wife and kids—and there were a lot of them— Mr. Johnson plopped down on the sofa and began helping himself to the sandwiches. Right away he broke one of Miss Mouse's china plates.

"Save some for me, ya big lug!" yelled Mrs. Johnson. "Don't make a rat of yourself!"

And finding that terribly amusing, they all laughed loudly. Little bits of cucumber and watercress sandwiches were spewed about the room. And one of the kids broke a teacup.

"What is this stuff?" he said, peering into the teapot. "Yucko."

Miss Mouse was outraged.

"I think you'd better leave," she said.

"Leave?" cried Mrs. Johnson. "We're gonna stay for dinner!"

Suddenly the tomcat stepped into the room.

The Johnsons' beedy little red eyes nearly popped out of their heads.

"Holy cow!" they cried. "She's got a bodyguard!"

And stumbling all over themselves they raced for the door, down the sidewalk, and into the hot rod. And they tore off.

Miss Mouse looked at the mess and sighed.

"I hope you've learned something," she said to the tomcat. "That was not a large family of mice, but a family of large *rats.* There *is* a difference!"

"So I see," said the tomcat.

And just to be sweet he made dinner that night and brought it to Miss Mouse in bed.

Fair-weather Pig

Have you heard about Pig?" asked the pharmacist.

"Oh no, what *now*?" said the barber, who'd come into the drugstore to get a prescription filled.

"He has a new job," said the pharmacist. "It's his fourth this month."

"It wasn't *always* Pig's fault that he kept getting fired," said the baker, who was buying toiletries. "Imagine hiring Pig to be an assistant chef! Monsieur Marcel had to close down for two whole days. There wasn't a morsel of food left in the kitchen."

"Then there was that job delivering groceries," said the pharmacist. "Same problem. None of the delivery orders got delivered. Pig had a picnic all by himself in the town square."

"And *then* he was hired to operate the merry-go-round in the park," said the baker. "But he couldn't resist shifting into high speed. Little kids had trouble staying on. The mayor fired Pig personally."

"This new job may work out," said the pharmacist. "No food about, no fast engines. Let's see how Pig's doing—it's about that time."

He switched on the television set above the cash register.

"And now for Mr. P and the weather," said the announcer.

"Oh my gosh," said the barber. "It's Pig. He's the new weather person."

"Hello," said Pig, looking directly at the camera. "Let's check the national weather."

With a long stick Pig pointed to the West Coast on the weather map.

"In Chicago it is hot and humid today."

"He's got it all wrong," said the barber. "He's pointing to San Francisco."

"Maybe Pig never studied geography," said the pharmacist.

"Pig quit school," said the baker. "Said he knew everything already."

"Shocking," said the pharmacist.

"My, my," said Pig. "What are these little white things doing all over the board? I'll just get rid of them."

And he removed all the snowflakes that were blanketing Texas.

"In that part of the country it will be clear and warm—I'm absolutely certain of it," said Pig.

"Oh dear," said the pharmacist. "Pig

isn't really cut out for this line of work. He's too imprecise."

"And now for the local weather," said Pig. "Get out your slickers, your umbrellas, and your rubber boots—it's gonna rain all week. I feel it in my bones."

The next day folks in town went to their jobs and schools wearing their rainy day clothes. As the day was sunny and hot, they all nearly melted. Many of them grumbled about the incompetent new weather person.

"The morning paper announced that he'd been fired," someone said.

"Have you heard about Pig?" said the baker a few days later.

"Yes," said the barber. "He was fired."

"Not that," said the baker. "Pig has a *new* job. Come have a look."

The barber hung up an "I'll be right

back" sign in his window and followed the baker. They were joined by the pharmacist. At Maple and Oak they came to Pig's little home on the hill. The place was crawling with little kids—climbing up the hill, squealing and zooming down the mud slide in front of Pig's house.

"That'll be another nickel," said Pig to one kid.

"Don't we ever get a free slide?" said the kid.

"Certainly not," said Pig. "This is a business."

"However did you think of it, Pig?" said the barber.

"Just one of my brainstorms," said Pig.

But the truth was that Pig had left the dishwater running when he'd gone to answer the phone and had forgotten all about it while he chattered away with Miss Lola. It was only when he felt his feet all wet that he realized what had happened. The sink had overflowed; dishwater had poured through the house, out the front door, and down Pig's hill—and had created the most magnificent mud slide in the county.

"You should be very proud, Pig," said the barber. "You have a fine business here."

Pig let his friends glide down the magnificent slide for half price. Then he helped himself to a ride.

"Hotcha!" he cried out.

And down he zoomed.

When Pig
Got Smart

When Pig's slippery slide went out of business (parents had not been amused with their kids coming home covered in mud from head to toe), Pig went out to look for other employment.

"I have lots of bills," Pig said to the barber.

"Have you had any nibbles for a job?" asked the barber.

"I saw a sign in the window of the candy shop for a salesperson," said Pig.

"Most unsuitable, Pig," said the baker, who was having his ears combed out. "You mustn't be around anything too tempting."

"You're right," said Pig.

"I've got it!" said the pharmacist. "It says here in the paper that the Board of Education is advertising for a truant officer. Seems that kids aren't showing up for school in record numbers."

"What's a truant officer?" said Pig.

"Someone who tracks down kids who are playing hooky," said the barber.

"It will just be like hide-and-seek," said Pig. "I'm sure I'd be good at it. I'll apply right away."

He hurried out of the barbershop and went off to be interviewed at the Board of Ed.

"No one else wants the job," whispered the Head of the Board to the other members. "We might as well give it to Pig."

The others agreed.

"The job is yours, Pig. Good luck."

Pig was overjoyed. It hadn't taken him long to find a job.

I just have the knack, he thought.

"Then it's all settled," said the Head of the Board. "You'll begin first thing tomorrow. Report to the Watson School at eight o'clock sharp."

"Beg pardon?" said Pig. "Do you mean eight A.M.? I'm a late sleeper. Eleven would suit me much better."

"Eight A.M.," said the Head, removing his glasses. "Of course if you don't *want* the job . . ."

"I'll be there at eight," said Pig.

That night Pig set his alarm clock for seven forty-five the next morning.

"I'll have to rush," said Pig. "But I'll get a bit more sleep."

At eight o'clock the next morning he appeared at the Watson School. He'd slept in his clothes, and they were all rumpled.

"The principal will see you now," said Miss Gomez, the secretary.

Pig knocked on the principal's door.

"Enter," said the principal. "Ah, Pig, your first day on the job. It's going to be a tough one."

"May I take two hours off for lunch?" said Pig.

"No," said the principal.

Gosh, thought Pig, this *is* going to be a tough job.

For several days Pig looked for kids playing hooky, but he couldn't find any. Then one day in the park he saw a young dog sitting on a bench, reading a book.

"Shouldn't you be in school?" said Pig.

"Nope," said the young dog, completely absorbed in his book.

"And why not?" said Pig.

"I know everything already," said the young dog, turning the page of his book.

"I see," said Pig.

He decided to be clever.

"Oh, yeah, Mr. Smarty?" he said. "So what is the capital of Miami?"

The young dog put down his book.

"Miami is a city," he said. "It is in the state of Florida. And the capital of Florida is Tallahassee."

"Oh," said Pig. "I knew that."

The young dog went back to his reading. But Pig had not given up.

"If you're so smart," he said, "what's seventy-two times twelve?"

"Eight hundred and sixty-four," said the young dog.

"How did you do that so quickly?" said Pig.

"Brains," said the young dog.

"Well, you can always learn something in school," said Pig. "You might become even smarter."

"Not today," said the young dog.

"And just why not?" said Pig.

"Because it's Saturday!" cried the young dog.

And he ran off howling with laughter.

"Have you heard about Pig?" asked the barber.

"Oh no, he got fired again?" said the pharmacist.

"Not exactly," said the barber. "Pig was so ashamed by all the things he didn't know that he's gone back to school."

"Well, maybe Pig is smarter than we thought," said the pharmacist.

Rats on
the Range

When the Waldo Rat family boarded the bus in New York City for the Far West, they were in pretty bad shape. Mrs. Rat was skinny and pale. Her tail was bandaged in three places where it had been stepped on by clumsy pedestrians. Waldo Rat's paws shook so badly that he could barely lift the tin suitcase up into the bus—the suitcase that contained all their worldly goods.

"I've lived here all my life," said Grannie Rat. "But I'm not sorry to be leaving. Life in the big city is just too strenuous. And the food has gotten simply inedible."

Little Floyd was not unhappy to be

leaving either. There were a lot of mean bullies in his neighborhood, and he was always having to defend himself.

Little Wanda, the baby, didn't know *what* to think.

"All aboard!" called out the bus driver.

The Rats settled into their seats for the long ride to the West and said good-bye to New York.

"We might come back for a visit," said Waldo. "If things improve."

Meanwhile, way out West, a yellow dog (a rat terrier to be precise) was sweeping out the bunkhouse at his ranch. To make extra money Tom Terrier and his wife had turned their property into a dude ranch—a place where city slickers could come to escape the big city, enjoy the fresh open air, and eat excellent, healthy meals. The Rats of New York were to be their first customers.

"We'll have to fatten them up," said Tom Terrier, giving his wife a look.

"I'll find something in my recipe book," said his wife, who knew perfectly well what that look signified.

Several days later the cross-country bus dropped the Rats at the gate of the dude ranch. They had not slept well on the trip, had deep circles under their eyes, and were nervous and jittery.

"Well, here we are!" sang out Waldo Rat in as cheerful a voice as he could manage. "What a lovely spot."

But it wasn't really so lovely—just flat rocky land, no trees, and only a few scruffy bushes.

"I'm going back to New York," said Mrs. Rat.

"Give it a chance," said her husband.

A cloud of dust appeared on the horizon, and they soon made out a jeep coming toward them.

"Welcome to the Bar T Ranch!" said Tom Terrier. "You must be the Rats."

Mrs. Rat all but fainted.

"Er," said Waldo. "In your letter you failed to mention you were a rat terrier."

"I'm a vegetarian," said Tom Terrier.

He was lying.

With some trepidation the Rats climbed into the jeep. As the next bus was not due for several days, they had no other choice. And they were tired and hungry.

Mrs. Tom Terrier welcomed them at the door of the ranch house.

"I'm a vegetarian," she said.

The Rats were delighted to have the bunkhouse to themselves.

"I wouldn't relish sleeping under the same roof as a rat terrier," said Grannie.

"They seem nice enough," said Mrs. Rat.

That night the Rats went to bed early, slept all night and into the next day. When they awoke, Mrs. Terrier had prepared a big country-style meal—Southern fried chicken, mashed potatoes, hot buttered biscuits. The Rats gobbled it all up, asked for seconds, and then asked for thirds.

"She uses too much salt," whispered Grannie.

Days went by and the Rats' health and nerves improved considerably. Tom noticed that they were putting on weight. And the horses noticed it as well. Every morning the Rats went for their ride around the corral. And every morning the horses got slower and slower—until they refused to budge.

"Those rats are eating us out of house

and home," said Mrs. Terrier to her husband. "We're not making any money."

"I'll think of something," said Tom Terrier, giving his wife one of those "You-know-what-I-mean" looks.

"Oh," said his wife.

But something occurred during the night that proved astounding. When Waldo Rat awoke, he noticed that his legs and feet were sticking out beyond the bedposts. The same was true with Grannie, Mrs. Rat, Floyd, and baby Wanda, who was huge. Mrs. Terrier's cooking and all the healthy air had really gone to work.

"We've grown!" cried Mr. Rat.

"So I see," said his wife. "It must have been all that home cooking."

When Tom Terrier saw the Rats coming in for breakfast, he nearly dropped dead. They were the biggest rats he'd ever seen.

"Good morning," said Waldo Rat. "We're hungry!"

"Coming right up," said Mrs. T., who went to the kitchen to rustle up some grub.

Tom Terrier couldn't help but feel that the Rats had grown even more while they were eating. Mr. Rat bumped his head on the door frame as he left the ranch house.

"They've gotten too big," said Tom to his wife. "We'll go broke if they stay."

"Their month is almost up," said his wife.

Waldo Rat came to the door.

"Good news," he said. "We've decided to stay another month. We're so happy here. Our health is much improved."

"So I see," said Tom Terrier.

There was no arguing with a six-foot rat. Tom said that he and his wife would be overjoyed to have the Rats stay on.

At dinner the Rats noticed that the portions were on the skimpy side.

"More candied yams, please," said Floyd.

But there weren't any more.

The next day Mrs. Terrier took the last of her savings and went into town for supplies.

"They're the biggest rats I've ever seen," she said to the grocer.

"You're joking," said the grocer.

"Six feet tall and then some," said Mrs. T.

"My, my," said the grocer. "I'd pay to see *that!*"

"Me too," said a shopper.

"Oh, really," said Mrs. T.

At first the Terriers had a hard time persuading the Rats to exhibit themselves.

"We don't want to be on display," said Grannie.

Her stomach began to grumble.

"Think of all those homecooked meals we'll be able to afford," said Mrs. T.

And the Rats agreed to do it.

That afternoon Tom Terrier removed the Bar T Ranch sign over the gate of the ranch and replaced it with "Prehistoric Rat Range—admission Fifty Cents." Folks from miles around came to have a look. The Rats were even persuaded to dress up in Western duds. And Grannie Rat became so stagestruck that she did a little dance for the customers.

Buzzard's Will

When old Buzzard Watkins appeared to be on his last legs, friends and relatives he hadn't seen in years came to pray at his bedside.

"Poor old Buzzard," said his nephew Clyde. "He was my favorite uncle."

"I'll cry for him for months and months," said Aunt Rose.

"For years and years!" said the barber, who'd been called in to give Buzzard a last shave.

"Poor Buzzard, poor poor Buzzard," cried everyone.

"Good riddance!" said Rooster Calhoun, who never liked Buzzard Watkins.

They lived across the road from each other and had never hit it off.

"What if he leaves you a little something in his will?" said the barber.

"I never thought of *that*!" said Rooster. "Do you think he might?"

"He has gobs of money," said Clyde the nephew. "You never can tell."

Old Buzzard opened his one good eye, looked about the room, heaved a deep sigh, and closed his eye.

"He's gone," said Aunt Rose.

"Where's that will?" cried Rooster Calhoun. "It must be somewhere here in the house!"

The friends and relatives dashed around opening drawers and chests, turning vases upside down. Chairs and side tables got knocked over. Papers flew about.

"It's not here!" said Aunt Rose. "It's just not here!"

"Wait a minute," said Rooster. "What's that sticking out from underneath the pillow?"

Rooster pulled out a scroll of paper.

"The will!" he cried.

And everyone huddled around him.

"I hope I get the house," said Clyde.

"Surely he'll leave me all the jewelry," said Aunt Rose. "He loved me so."

"I could use some money," said the barber. "After all, I shaved him for years."

Rooster Calhoun dropped the will and stared into space.

"Nobody here gets anything," he said. "Buzzard Watkins has left all his money, his house, and all his personal possessions to the Society for Stray Cats!"

"Why, that horrid old thing!" cried Aunt Rose. "How selfish of him!"

"He was probably feeling guilty for all his wicked ways," said Clyde.

"We've been robbed!" cried the others.

Rooster Calhoun scratched his beak and was lost in thought.

"Hush," said Aunt Rose. "Rooster Calhoun is thinking."

A silence fell on the room.

"I may have a solution," said Rooster. "But it will require your help."

"We'll help," said the others.

"What," said Rooster, "if there was another will, leaving *us* everything?"

"Impossible," said Clyde. "This one is dated yesterday."

"Nevertheless," said Rooster. "There *could* be a newer one."

"But Uncle Buzzard is *dead*," said Clyde. "He can't sign a new will."

"Don't worry," said Rooster. "I have a plan."

And old Buzzard Watkins was removed to the guest room.

That afternoon the lawyer Foxworth came to call.

"Poor Uncle Buzzard is on his last legs," said Clyde. "You'll hardly recognize him."

"Take me to him," said the lawyer Foxworth.

Clyde led the lawyer into Buzzard Watkins's bedroom. Around the bed the friends and relatives were on their knees praying. The lawyer could not get close to the bed.

"Look, Uncle Buzzard," said Clyde. "Here's lawyer Foxworth. You asked to see him, remember?"

From the bed there came a soft wheezing sound. Rooster Calhoun stuck out a shaky wing toward the lawyer.

"Not too close," he said. "It could be contagious."

"You wished to see me, Buzzard?" said the lawyer.

"Ah yes," said Rooster in his most gravelly Buzzard Watkins voice. "I've had a change of heart. I want to alter my will— in favor of everyone here."

"You're too kind!" cried out Aunt Rose.

The lawyer unrolled a blank piece of paper he'd brought along.

"Very well," he said. "You will dictate and I will write it all down."

"First of all," said Rooster, "I wish to leave something to dear Aunt Rose. She will receive my cuff links."

"Awk!" cried Aunt Rose, clutching her heart.

"To my nephew Clyde," continued Rooster, "I bequeath my riding boots and saddle."

"What!" cried Clyde.

"And to the others," said Rooster, "I leave one dollar apiece."

"What?!" cried the others.

But they could say no more. Tampering with a will is a serious offense and they could get into big trouble.

"That leaves the house and all the rest of the money," said the lawyer Foxworth.

"Ah yes," said Rooster. "I almost forgot. Those I leave to my beloved and cherished friend, Rooster Calhoun."

"Sign here," said the lawyer.

Rooster Calhoun made an "X" at the end of the will.

"You've been most helpful," he said to the lawyer. "Now if you'll leave me to my prayers."

"Of course," said lawyer Foxworth. And he left.

The friends and relatives were furious.

"You tricked us!" they cried.

"You will kindly leave my house this instant!" said Rooster Calhoun. "Or I'll have to summon the authorities."

With much grumbling the friends and relatives began to leave. Suddenly the door flew open, and there stood Buzzard Watkins.

"So!" cried Buzzard. "What a lot of scheming, conniving thieves I see before me!"

"But, but . . . ," said the others.

"I was only pretending!" said Buzzard. "Only pretending."

"Rats!" said Rooster.

And he stormed out.

"Rats!" said the others, following on his heels.

They knew they'd never get a single penny from old Buzzard now.

But no matter—Buzzard Watkins lived another fifteen years. And he did not leave his money to the Society for Stray Cats after all. He spent it all on himself. And what a fine time he had too.